No Spots for
this Giraffe!

Papineau, Lucie
(Pas de taches pour une girafe. English)
No spots for this giraffe!
(The adventures of Gilda)
Translation of: Pas de taches pour une girafe.

ISBN 1-903582-24-5
In English for Europe
© 2002 Merlin Publishing, Ireland
All rights reserved.

© Les éditions Héritage inc. 1999
All rights reserved.
Published by permission of Les éditions Héritage inc.,
St-Lambert, Quebec, Canada.

Printed in Canada
10 9 8 7 6 5 4 3 2 1

Merlin Publishing
16 Upper Pembroke Street
Dublin 2
Ireland

Tel: (353-1) 6764373
Fax: (353-1) 6764368
E-mail: publishing@merlin.ie
Web site: www.merlin-publishing.com

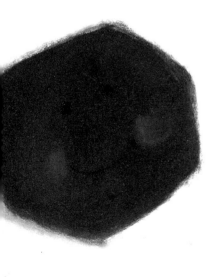

Text: Lucie Papineau

Illustrations: Marisol Sarrazin

English Text: Sheila Fischman

*For my brother André,
who loves melons.* L.P.

No Spots for
this Giraffe!

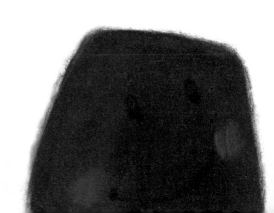

MERLIN PUBLISHING

Like every giraffe in the world, Gilda is covered with spots.
From her head to her feet and all down her long neck.
That's a lot of spots!

But when the North Wind blows Whoosh! Whoosh! the spots all fly away like
hundreds of butterflies with no heads or tails.
And that's why Gilda is the only giraffe in the world who lives in a cave.

Now luckily, in the land where giraffes live, the North Wind is usually in bed. But if, as bad luck should have it, he wakes up... all of Gilda's spots cry out: "Run for your life! Here comes the North Wind!"

And lickety-split, the little giraffe runs off to her cave. The North Wind would never go that far to look for her...

"Whew!" the giraffe and her spots shouted together. "That was a close call!"

The spots, relieved, burst out laughing. They laugh so hard that Gilda cannot hear the song of the wind. But still it keeps blowing and blowing...

"Now then," thinks the little giraffe, always ready for a snack, "all is well. Next stop, my favourite field of melons!" But as soon as she gets there, Whoosh! The North Wind takes away her spots...

"NO!" howls Gilda.

She cries so loud that the North Wind, dazed, stops blowing all at once.

And poof! Her spots are scattered here and there, all over the land of the giraffes and even beyond.

Gilda is very angry.

"I won't give up looking for my spots until I find them all," she says. "And if I can't find them, I will never touch a beautiful round melon again!"

Poor Gilda goes deep into the jungle, then farther and farther in.
She shivers from loneliness. She can't see her spots anywhere.

Timothy the tiger was passing by. He felt his heart melt exactly like an icy melon in the sun.

"Stop shivering, Gilda. I'll lend you my striped robe. It will keep you warm, you'll see!"

For a few seconds the little giraffe is perfectly happy. But then a worried frown creases her brow.

"Timothy, Timothy, what can you be thinking? Stripes make me look terribly fat! Your robe is much prettier on you, believe me."

And the clothes-conscious giraffe continues on her way through the vines.

Without her spots, she shivers in dismay.

When Lancelot the leopard sees her like this, it brings tears to his eyes.
He decides to lend her his spots. And he even lets her have his whiskers too!

Gilda sighs happily. She is all wrapped up in his soft spots. But the more she sighs, the more her new whiskers prickle and tickle her!

"Achoo! Achoo! It was sweet of you to lend me your spots, Lancelot... But whiskers, really, they aren't for me! Achoo!"

And the little giraffe, who is allergic to whiskers, continues on her way through the bamboo. She shivers unhappily.

Papaya the giant panda catches sight of her. Right away he stops chewing bamboo. The little giraffe looks so unhappy that he can't eat anymore. And without a word he covers Gilda with his own soft fur.

Now Gilda isn't unhappy at all. She smoothes her new coat and munches a little bamboo. She even performs a few pirouettes.

Then she starts to feel hot... so terribly hot that she'd rather just go naked again!

And the naked little giraffe continues on her way to
the edge of the big lake. She shivers in gloom...

Underwater, the multicoloured fish beckon to her.

"Come and swim with us! Don't stay all by yourself..."

Gilda dives into the ocean and tries on the glittering robes of the fish.
She takes part in their great water ballet.

Head up, head down, head to one side... Soon Gilda feels seasick!

So the seasick little giraffe goes back to the grasslands and continues along her way. She shivers with sadness.

Nearby, Zephyr the zebra is playing Zorro. He feels very brave. He sees Gilda shivering and immediately takes off his coat.

Gilda smiles sweetly in her new pajamas.

"That's so kind of you, Zephyr. All my friends are so kind...

But I want my spots, my own spots! They're so soft and so much fun..."

And the little giraffe continues along her way, farther and farther, still shivering. All the way to the foot of an unfamiliar hill.

Corazon the chameleon is sitting on a rock, changing his colour (that's his job).

"Here you are! I've been waiting for you, little giraffe."

"Oh no! Don't tell me you're going to lend me your robe too," says Gilda. "My head will turn into a melon if I change colour again..."

"Not at all, dear, not at all! Look what I've got for you."

"Oh! It's my spot!" Gilda exclaims. "My own pretty, soft, funny spot!"

"Hurray!" exclaims the spot. "It's my giraffe!"

And Gilda the giraffe, her eyes shining, puts her funny spot back where it belongs.

In the distance she hears the voices of all her friends, as if she were dreaming:

"Yoo-hoo, Gilda! Where are you? We've found your spots... The little rascals, they were hiding in our coats!"

Now that everything is back to normal (well, almost), there is just one thing that Gilda wants. All her friends are invited to a great banquet – of beautiful round melons!

Let's hope that the North Wind prefers cucumbers...